*For Mamouchka and Bon-Papà*
Q. G.

Copyright © 2003 by Nord-Süd Verlag AG, Gossau Zürich, Switzerland
First published in Switzerland under the title *Du bist die liebste kleine Maus!*
English translation copyright © 2004 by North-South Books Inc., New York

All rights reserved. No part of this book may be reproduced or utilized in any form or by
any means, electronic or mechanical, including photocopying, recording, or any information
storage and retrieval system, without permission in writing from the publisher.

First published in the United States, Great Britain, Canada, Australia, and New Zealand in 2004
by North-South Books, an imprint of Nord-Süd Verlag AG, Gossau Zürich, Switzerland.
Distributed in the United States by North-South Books Inc., New York.

Library of Congress Cataloging-in-Publication Data is available.
A CIP catalogue record for this book is available from The British Library.
ISBN 0-7358-1890-8 (trade edition)
1 3 5 7 9 HC 10 8 6 4 2
ISBN 0-7358-1891-6 (library edition)
1 3 5 7 9 LE 10 8 6 4 2
Printed in Italy
For more information about our books, and the authors and artists
who create them, visit our web site: www.northsouth.com

# The Dearest Little Mouse in the World

By Antonie Schneider

Illustrated by
Quentin Gréban

Translated by J. Alison James

North-South Books
New York · London

Every day little Fay said good-bye to her mother
and set off to school with her friends.

Every day little Fay walked past a big, black dog.

"Hello!" the dog barked, every single day.

But Fay just walked past. She never even noticed him.

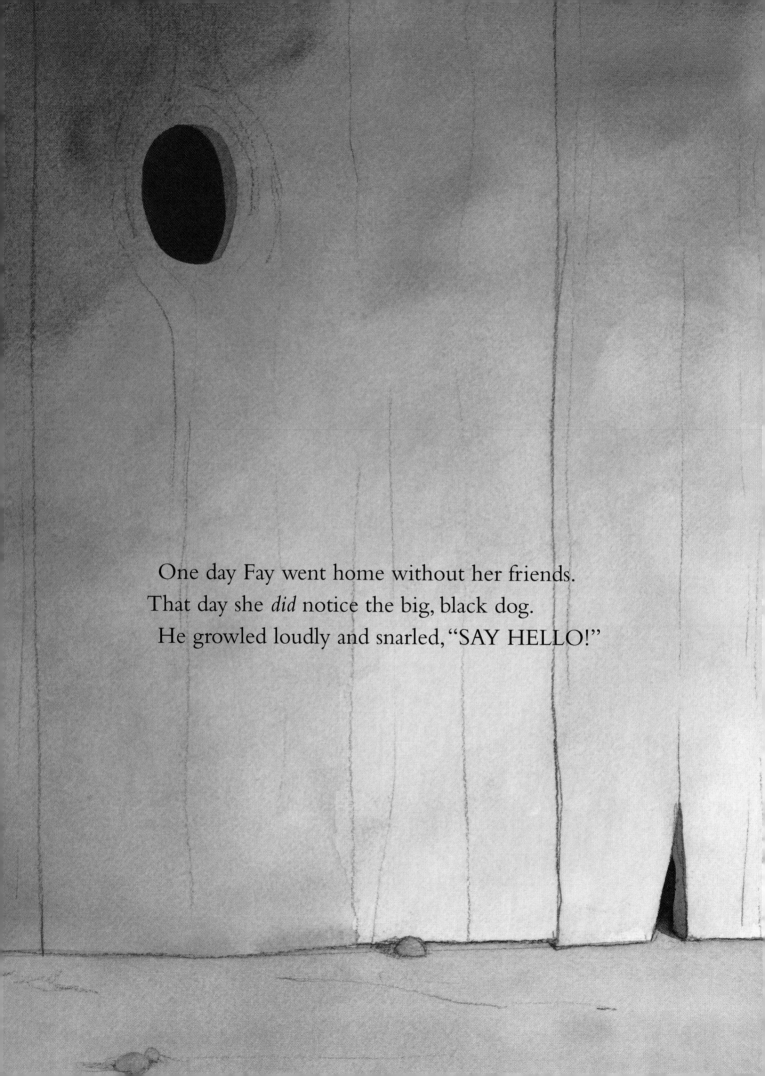

One day Fay went home without her friends.
That day she *did* notice the big, black dog.
He growled loudly and snarled, "SAY HELLO!"

Fay was so frightened she ran all the way home.

Her mother and father were waiting for her.

"Would you like some bacon, Fay?" her mother asked.

"No!" said Fay.

"How about a piece of cheese?" asked her father.
Fay shook her head.

Fay said no to chocolate pudding.
She even said no to grapes.
"Whatever is wrong with our little Fay?" asked
her mother.

"I hate the big, black dog," Fay said, scowling.

"Why?" asked her father.

"He growled at me. He scared me."

"What did he say?" asked her father.

Fay had to think. Then she replied in a loud, growling voice, "Say hello!"

Her father laughed. "I think I understand," he said. "The black dog just wants to be your friend!"

"Why would he want to be my friend?" Fay asked. "I'm just a little mouse."

Her father dragged the big mirror in from the
bedroom. "Look and see," he said.

"See what?" asked Fay.

"See what a lovely little mouse you are," her mother
said.

"The dearest little mouse in the world," said her
father. "Of course he wants to be your friend."

"This is what I think happened," her father said.
"Every day you walk right past him on your way to
school. Every day he barks a friendly hello to you.
But you never say hello back. Am I right?"

Fay sat very still. "You are right," she agreed.
Then she had an idea. She took a piece of bacon
and ran out of the house.

Bravely, little Fay stood before the fence. "I've brought you something," she said.

"Wow!" said the big, black dog, and he licked his chops. Then he gobbled up the bacon. "Thank you!" he said. "You are a lovely little mouse. I'm sorry I frightened you."

"I *was* scared," said Fay. "But not anymore. I know you were just trying to be friends."

Now every day, when little Fay is on her way to school, she says "Hello!" to the big, black dog.

And every day on her way back home, she stops for a while to play.

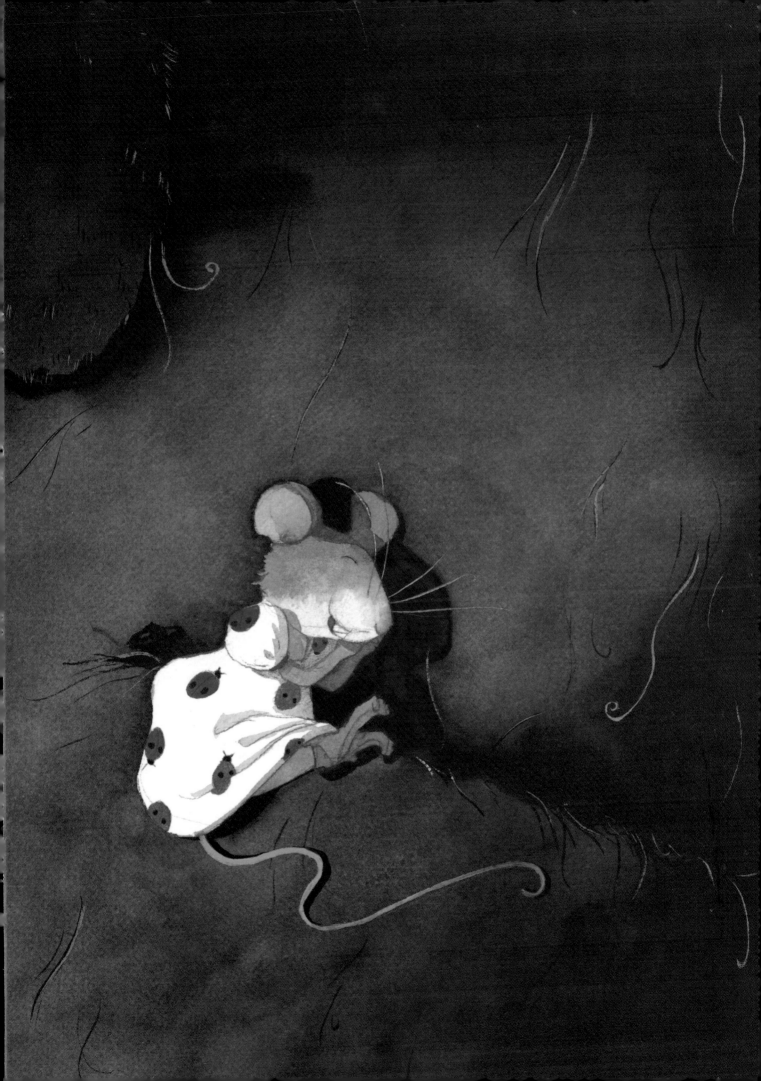